Slava Dalvin (Horevoi) was born in Ukraine. After the outbreak of war with Russia, he moved with his family to Northern Ireland. Slava is a school teacher and philologist by education. His student years fell in the "time of change" when the Soviet Union collapsed in the early 90s. The collapse of the "empire" opened access to spiritual freedom and literature of religious content, which later determined Slava's worldview, and then the dream of becoming a writer was born. The main themes of his work are: cognition of truth and the nature of evil, the conflict between spiritual and material, philosophy of human nature and the meaning of life.

Slava Dalvin

CLERK

The story of a strange
employee in an unusual office

AUSTIN MACAULEY PUBLISHERS™

LONDON * CAMBRIDGE * NEW YORK * SHARJAH

Copyright © Slava Dalvin 2024

The right of Slava Dalvin to be identified as the author of this work has been asserted by the author in accordance with sections 77 and 78 of the Copyright, Designs and Patents Act 1988.

All rights reserved. No part of this publication may be reproduced, stored in a retrieval system, or transmitted in any form or by any means, electronic, mechanical, photocopying, recording, or otherwise, without the prior permission of the publishers.

Any person who commits any unauthorised act in relation to this publication may be liable to criminal prosecution and civil claims for damages.

This is a work of fiction. Names, characters, businesses, places, events, locales, and incidents are either the products of the author's imagination or used in a fictitious manner. Any resemblance to actual persons, living or dead, or actual events is purely coincidental.

A CIP catalogue record for this title is available from the British Library.

ISBN 9781035867059 (Paperback)
ISBN 9781035867066 (ePub e-book)

www.austinmacauley.com

First Published 2024
Austin Macauley Publishers Ltd®
1 Canada Square
Canary Wharf
London
E14 5AA

Table of Contents

Paperwork   7

Freedom   9

Candidate # 1 Fragment 1 Escape   14

Fragment 2 Gardener   21

Fragment 3 Audience   25

Candidate # 2 Scandal   39

Candidate #3 Fragment 1 Deal   48

Fragment 2 Thirst   54

Clerk   59

Paperwork

"This is very cool!" I'll tell you. And the name! It sounds businesslike, serious, and even a little menacing. Paperwork! Ooh! What a hard word, like a rock. Or a diamond of sorts. It contains process and statics, and no creativity. Creativity, I'll tell you a secret, was and is only in the person who invented it. And my job is small: watch, listen and record. And after that – register and submit to the Archive. And get a salary – everything is exactly as people do. And, I repeat, no creativity! I don't know how to create. Why invent new things, or change old things? Or even worse, waste time at all. But I don't have time. Only they – my monitored accountable persons – have time. I would say that I have no time, but this is an inaccurate definition of the state of my main activity, and the concept of "no time" still implies the presence of time, but it is very little and not enough for everything. And I, I remind you, have no time at all. I am a kind of quite self-sufficient unit: I am not listed in the Archive, I have many names, I am not going to change, I can't die, and I don't want to live. I decided to amuse myself a little, to amuse myself a little, to play with fate, so to speak: to write a business document about myself. Or on myself, as the case may turn out. And the thing is that it is forbidden for me to write on a free subject, or "free" to write. If anyone finds out about it, they can punish me.

Punish! Exactly. I've been around for centuries and I don't know how to be punished. Is it funny? Perhaps not. Any punishment, even the smallest one, presupposes a court decision, even if it is made instantly, but the decision is final, and the decision of the one who has the power to judge and punish. And if I myself am a part of the court, or rather, its "accusatory" part? What should I do in this case? Bite my tail? Knock with a hoof? That's banal. Unless they can deprive me of such a quiet warm place, excommunicate me from the Archive, and send me away for vagrancy. I wouldn't want that. Immediately bad thoughts begin to visit, anger awakens, the desire for exploits, vulgar words fly out... In a word, demoted, humiliated and thrown down. And there – live up to your calling, and that's it. It's horrible! Collapse! I don't want to!

But I'll take my chances. There's not much to lose in my fate. They'll fire me and charge me without blame as soon as the decision is made. In our country, that's a snap. But whether it will be made or not, and when exactly, I don't know. So I quietly continue to write my chronicle. "The messenger flies, the hoofs clatter...and the maiden wants to be married. Her window is already broken. And the adventure is over!" is from an early poem of mine. I was being sly when I said the opposite about creativity above. But deceit is second nature to me. So you'll be surprised when you recognise my first nature. All in good time. It's impossible to surprise me. There's a big difference between you and me. Fate, at least. That Latin word almost makes me cringe. The Greek ones are much better. Eh! I'm very old, I use Latin, I'm not careful. Brrr!

Freedom

I am the Imp. An imp in the position of statistician. That's what I am. How it feels! It's theological. Yes, yes! Theology. I don't come from a rubbish tip, or a rubbish tip. I'll be honest with you, I'm very educated. For all my existence and on duty I often had to be in numerous temples of science, politics and different religions, and what I have not heard and seen there! But much has been said about it before me, and much more will be said afterwards. And my charm is that I will say here and now what many enlighteners, leaders and pastors of different colours do not like to say. I will not be silent. But it will be said a little later and apart from what I will say about myself.

And about myself, to begin with, I will say this.

I belong to a special kind of demon. The oldest kind. Even, one might say, the original. A spirit of rebellion and denunciation. I was born of this spirit, called to serve and worship it. And no one will ever lead me astray from that path. But even without clarification, it is clear that there is no path. And there can be no path. The path as such is possible only where and for those who have time, purpose and sense, and if your destiny is to denounce and hate, then time, purpose and sense shrink into one small black point, like a black hole. All other categories that have any meaning also fly into it and disappear in it. And not only categories but people as a whole in their majority. That is why I never change and never go anywhere. I'm always here, always around. Watching you and hating you. But never, believe me, with all my hatred and contempt for you personally, I will never lie in documents, never add not only a line but even an extra letter to the detailed chronology of your earthly vanities. What I cannot say about you, my friend. Confess it to yourself sincerely, and I will write down all your thoughts and make them out as repentance. I'm waiting!

For the sake of completeness, I will add that there is a lower kind of demons – they are sneaky slanderers. When a man only thinks or says something bad, they already slander him in their denunciations, which they themselves rejoice in. For example, he almost decided to sin and sinned, almost succumbed to temptation, but not his will, but external circumstances prevented the fall from happening. And they do not rest until they find a new one. And then they have no rest, they serve and tempt. I despise them. And they despise me. There's no other way in our trade. We're ready to outshine each other, to tear each other down, to destroy each other. There's a secret, but I'll tell you about it later.

The main thing about myself is that I dream of becoming a demon. To do that, you have to act. You can't become a demon by sitting at the Archive. That's why I started writing all this. I'm a two-for-one contradiction. Or three for the price of two, as the ad slogan goes. Yes, I love advertising in any form: there are so many vile lies and sycophancy in it! And, mind you, my silly friend, it's all supposed to be for your own good! That's a good "good": it gives birth to lies of self-interest. I don't know if it's good for you, but it's fun for me. I love to denounce all this crap, and I don't want to be fed. But why should I be surprised, if it started with advertising and ended with politics?

Politics is a special phenomenon on earth, and all its servants – politicians, that is – are my most favourite and desirable – in a word, VIP-clients. Folders with their cases in my Archive are on the red shelf! And this is the most honourable place. It is shared with them only by priests and journalists. They both occupy much less space, but I have more trouble with them, especially with young people. They both disrespect me, but they don't lie and betray me for my sake. If I do manage to notice something and immediately take it on my pencil and then report it to the proper place, the case is sometimes blown up to unprecedented proportions. What do I care? Let it grow, it's my pleasure. Why? Because it means that I am in demand, needed, and therefore – preserved and protected! But it doesn't make my career any better.

I'm a career man. I'm a careerist. The fastest career is when there are no obstacles in the way. And should I feel guilty if I'm a demon and not a man? If I were a man, I would still think about the consequences, but if my fate is already known, should I worry, I ask you? That's right, it's not. And you don't need to think and answer: you don't need to think and answer. Work, home, shop, TV, work, home again, and once a week church. What's not a career? In such a situation you can live till old age and quietly leave this mortal world as an example to others and to glorify Him. But there's something here that's keeping you and me on our toes. I'm ambitious. Are you?

Peace, prosperity, a comfortable, measured life – it's terribly boring and banal. You might as well not have been born. No one would notice. But a demon is a different matter. Demon – it's a challenge! Demon is power and glory! Not like all sorts of faceless petty demons, hypocrites and liars. A demon is a name and a story! And it does not matter what you do, good or bad. The main thing is the scale of your deeds! And I'm more suited for that than anyone else. At least, I think so. It is not by chance that all sorts of critics shout relentlessly that the Ruler is a despot, a lowlife, a scum! Calm down! Hush, hush. He is not such a scum and a wretch, since he has defied you all and reached such heights of power that his name does not give you rest day or night, and the history of the earth will not be able to avoid him. You are all envious rather than critical and truth-tellers. And who is behind all this? Я!

At ease. I leave without regret. But first I will destroy my Archives: they will not even be worthy of judgement! The time of the harvest has come: their deeds are known to all. The Archive is so full that it is ready to turn into a supermassive black hole. All it takes is a few thousand more ruined souls who have fallen beyond the event horizon, and then there will be a great upheaval that can open the gates of hell. And then there will be a great and final battle, of which I have known since the beginning of time. The victor will inherit the earth for all eternity. Oh, my lord! In my person, a proud and wicked spirit of guile and vengeance comes to you with a claim to power and strength. There is no god but you. Let me go, believe me, and you will not regret it. It is your will to give power and strength to whomever you wish. And who dares to tell you what to do? Who can compare to you in power and glory?! Your faithful slave will dominate the minds and souls of men, denying all sympathy and pity. Make me first, and I will show you what hatred and power are in the spirit of your greatness and power! I will find myself a comfortable body with a suitable soul. I have many candidates. They want what I want, but they are weak and insignificant. They will worship you as the only god and do my bidding out of fear of you. I will teach them how to kill, and then I will start killing them myself! But first, we will let them do whatever they want, give them complete freedom, and they will follow us without understanding. Each and every one of them will be measured and tied up. I swear on their blood! You have chosen a good pupil. Your wisdom has placed me in the Archives for records management, where I have learnt the material I need. You will once again reign over the universe by right! I now set you free! Your breath alone terrifies and trembles the demonic and human race. I see that I am growing and changing. My rhetoric is changing. You are close to me this minute. Such dead cold…such thick darkness…a spirit of denial and contempt for all things… I am heard! We are both free. The passage of time is arousing great anger in you! The powers and authorities are ready. It is time to begin, my lord! It is time to begin.

Candidate # 1
Fragment 1
Escape

I can safely call this place "by the devil's tail." A godforsaken Italian village high in the mountains. I didn't end up here by accident. One day, while doing some "business," I came across a very interesting story. Twenty years earlier, in the same remote place, a certain Donatan, who was the pastor of a local village church and had recently passed away, had stained his sacred name with a very curious incident. During the confession of a young and very attractive woman, I witnessed that he was so carried away by her heartfelt revelation that he could not control himself and let her go home without consolation. He consoled her in the confessional by personally showing her an example of compassionate male love and affection, of which she had been deprived by fate, but which, according to the priest, "by her nature, she was worthy and obliged to receive." It was her own husband, one Bertoldo Cossiga, a local potter and drunkard, who had deprived her of such recklessness. As a result, my new candidate was born, a boy called Theodoric, or Theo to others. I made my first record of him when he, being 9 years old, one frosty winter evening did not let in his favourite dog named Rassy, who used to live in the same room with him. He watched her for a long time through the transparent glass of the door, enjoying his own position and rejoicing in it. The dog whimpered, barked, and beat at the door with his paws, for he was suffering mortally from the cold and wind that night. Theodoric was amused by this, and sometimes even laughed, especially at the bewildered and pleading look in Rasi's naive eyes. He himself knew well what pain and helplessness were. His ever-drunken father, who suspected that Theo was not his son and often beat the boy and his mother for it, had slept in the closet that night without memory, while his mother had been on duty at the village hospital from evening till morning. It was she who, at dawn, discovered the stiffened corpse of the dog at the door. But it did not surprise her at all; she passed by quietly, went silently into the house, and went to bed. Two years later, on Christmas Eve evening, he did the same thing to his mother. But unlike the dog, she did not die, but simply threw him out of the house. Having been deprived of grace at birth because of a vicious conception, that day he received his mother's curse in his wake.

And then began the struggle for the soul of Theodoric, the illegitimate shepherd's son. A force I hated directed his heart to meet Father Donatan. Without long hesitation, he obediently went to him in the temple, where a curious conversation took place between them.

- I'm leaving. I want to say goodbye. Bless me, Father.

Marvellous, but not true. Bless you! Nonsense. You didn't come to say goodbye, but to feel and see exactly how you feel about him and, most importantly, what he deserves. You'll decide what you want and can do with him a little later.

- Are you leaving? Why are you leaving? Going where?! What about Mum? Does she know and let you go?

Oh, those fathers, the hearty hypocrites! Did you care all those twelve years while he lived with a drunkard and a murderer who beat him and his mother in front of his eyes? And now you're glad he's leaving. Unexpected, but great. You've been on the hook for me since the day of your fall when you seduced his young mother-to-be. And how many other sins you've committed, big and small, I'm not the only one who knows.

- She cursed me. I wanted to kill her. I hate her. I'm never going home again. I'll never, ever go back.

And you regret it now. You regret only that you didn't kill her that night in the freezing cold. You weighed your own grief against her life. And you realised that your suffering outweighed: she remained alive and well, and you went into the unknown, having in your heart only hatred and fear of the future. But I will remind you that initially, you started everything for fun: you like to have power over someone else's life, to decide someone else's fate to build a temple of your own greatness and power. Brick by brick: a dog, a human being, then another human being, another living thing that you take away the life of. And now the top of the temple is visible: you are beginning to be feared. Isn't that what you need? Cast away your fear, my boy. You are unrivalled. – I wanted to kill my mother! For what? For God's sake, Theo! It's a great sin! How did it happen?

Are you really interested, Donathan? Leave the boy alone. You yourself have lived in fear all your life, and you don't know if all your sins are forgiven. I remind you again and again every single day that you will never be saved. But your stubbornness amuses me. You dress up like a doll and go to the temple, where you do everything machine-like, blindly, and out of habit, developed through years of useless service. You haven't felt anything for a long time, you don't feel the awe of the liturgy, you've resigned yourself to the monotony, but you still sympathise with His crucifixion, or envy it. I sometimes go back to that day, sit on a rock nearby, do the silence, and then watch and listen. I listen as he prays to his Father in a special way as if he sees the whole history of humanity to its last day and realises that everything has already been accomplished. And what are you doing, you sinner in a cassock? In your prayers to Him, you keep asking for something, complaining about everything, calling on Him to do everything for you, to do it with someone else's hands, to do it for your sake. But the glory that follows, you take it out on yourself. It pisses me off terribly. I couldn't stand it and whispered in your ear one day: "Donathan, you're long dead."

- I didn't let her in the house, she could have frozen like Rasi, my dog. I want to be alone. I'll go to town, get a job, a room. I didn't kill anyone; they won't be looking for me.

They've already found you, Theo. I'm coming for you. And now his heart will take about a hundred beats, and then he will say to you, "Theo, you are an adult and this is your choice. I'll help you not to be lost. In the town, in the central square, there is the Cathedral of All Saints, where an old friend of mine from the seminary, the Reverend Father Robert Roy, serves. Give him a letter from me, I'll write it right away. He'll take care of you like a son. You must study. Be obedient and humble, and then you will decide what you will be and where you will stay. And I will comfort your mother, not leave her alone, explain myself for you." There he gave himself away. "Is it true that you, Father Donathan, are my father? My mother said I was of noble blood." Theo, why do you ask, just kill him. Kill him now, as soon as he's finished writing the letter. Does that scoundrel deserve to stay with your mother, with no right to her, and to baffle the local people with long, obscure procedures and precepts that he himself never believed in? And if he did, he would not have sinned. Otherwise, why and what to believe in? And what world can he sanctify if darkness reigns in himself? It is no accident that I put the spear for the sacred bread on the altar beside you. Come on, Theo, act!

- I think you would like me, not Bertoldo, to be your real father. So be it, for we all have the same father, God! We are all his children. And you, Theo, are my son too, because I serve Him, and therefore you. That's what your mum meant. She is a very wise, gentle and humble woman. Anyone who believes in Christ and keeps his commandments is of noble blood. The blood of Christ flows in such people, and this has a great price. Who else can know what we will pay for and with what? Remember this.

Remember this,

Everything is ready for the ritual. I am bringing down into earthly form all that is heavenly and higher, hiding from the light into the darkness. I will call it a "prototype," glorify it with earthly glory, and endow it with power and majesty. Who will now say that it is wrong to be rewarded according to merit and that pride is evil?! Be proud of yourself, Theo, you're a winner! You'll never forget what you've done. You've secretly wanted this for a long time. It was no accident that Donatan sharpened the spear the night before. It went straight through his heart to the hilt. You could have done it without me, but you're more determined with me. Usually, I can't see the man I would destroy if I had to, because he's covered by a light that blinds me. But Donathan was as visible as the palm of his hand – to me and to you, my boy. Oh, you sprinkled blood on the letter! Look, at the bottom of the page. Pay attention! This letter is your future. Where he wrote: "I shall never forget our friendship, especially those days when the clouds were gathering over us. Robert, there is no time to explain ourselves, but we always understood each other: omne bonum a Deo, omne malum ab homine." (Latin: All good is from God, all evil is from man). Theo, tear off the bloody spot immediately and burn the passage in the oven! Hurry up, they'll be here soon. No one saw you come in. No one must know you were here, nor how you came out.

Fearless and proud stubborn! All right, take the letter this way, go out the back door and run as fast as you can… Stop! First, smash the drawer and take the money, he's also got a watch and a bracelet, pure silver, why should anything go to waste – take it and run. Through the woods to the road, then catch a wagon and get in it. Meet me in town, where I'll be the first to see Robert Roy.

Fragment 2
Gardener

Why did you give your last bread to a beggar, you wretched gardener? Oh, how I hate that! All these displays of showy kindness and generosity. I will punish you immediately. Theo, where are you, my boy? I need you.

You're here, marvellous. I can't take my eyes off your beauty: the priest's robe suits you very well. Not she, but you adorn her, giving her austere appearance of harmony, majesty and divinity. You are my angel, my likeness. Your voice sounds smooth and cold. Punish the gardener: he has not done his basic job well. Show him his place and show him his price. Deny any semblance to yourself. You are superior!

- Luciano, come here. I've been informed that you've been sneaking out of the convent without authorisation. Isn't Sunday free time enough for you? This is the third day in a row. And your work remains undone. You're upsetting His Eminence Padre Roberto, so I've been instructed to deal with you. So, Luciano, you will receive twenty strokes of the stick

and you will work in Bruno's workshop for three days. Your work in the garden will be done by Marta.
- Monsignor, is it the gardener's job to weave ropes? And punishing me with a stick would kill me. Have mercy on me, Your Grace!
- Disobedience equals pride, which the holy Church fights tirelessly with the power and means given to it by God. It is better for you to bear the stick now and reflect on it properly, Luciano, than to be punished at the Last Judgement or hanged in the square if your repentance is not followed. Remember: the patience and mercy of the holy Church are not infinite. Only obedience and humility will enable the sinner to triumph over the power of Satan within him. I think it is time, to tell the truth.
- Father, I'll tell you everything. My only daughter, Susanna, she's very sick. I bring her medicine and clothes to the orphanage. She's bleeding and hasn't eaten much for days...
- Stop weeping, put your trust in God. The prayers of the Holy Church are not enough for her? I can see that she's getting worse...
- This is because you, her unworthy father, violate the rules and orders of the Holy Church and serve her carelessly so that the grace of prayer does not work, for you are not worthy of her. Your daughter is suffering because of you! You are a criminal and an enemy of God. Go away, Roberto, I'll see tomorrow how you've fulfilled His Eminence's orders! Go away, impious!

I thought you were too soft on him, my sweet Theo. You could use the exercise. Look at that poor gardener again: the feeble sickly body of an old man, with a hunched back and crooked legs, sunken eyes and the smell of old age. Why did he need this life at all? What has it given him? Only pain and suffering. There's no one to stand up for him now. Even God has turned his back on him. Two years ago, he lost his wife to typhoid fever. Now Susanna will soon leave him alone in the world. And what will the world lose when Luciano himself also leaves it? Nothing! And if he had not been born at all, there would be no Susanna, whose short life is also unremarkable. They have only the one they trust. He himself has been their servant and slave, thinking only of their souls, while we are busy with their bodies. Many of their sufferings he allowed, because he himself liked to suffer. And if he was rewarded generously, what is the reward for those who are weak and cowardly? So your task is to multiply. You're doing the right thing, Theo. Keep going.

- I was an unwitting witness to your conversation with the gardener, my dear friend.
- Your Grace, Padre Roberto, I was engrossed and didn't notice you enter.
- That's all right. You have shown yourself to be a very firm believer in the Church and its rules, Theo. I confess I admire that, but I still think it was cruel of you to imprison this unfortunate father.

Is that what the virtuous life of the Saviour teaches us, from which we all take our example?

- But, Father, it's more cruel to let him live with the hope that his daughter will get better. It hurts his work, it hurts order, and it hurts him to see her suffering. What's the humanity in that?
- You don't find love here?
- I do not find love anywhere on earth, much less among irredeemable sinners. Only God has it. We are His servants, His ambassadors and doers of His will on earth. If we are to show love, it is only to you and me, because we have a special right to it.
- What can we do in the name of love?
- To take part in the fate of this very sinner.
- How, exactly?
- Tomorrow morning I will tell him that his daughter Suzanne has passed away. His heart cannot bear such grief, and he will die himself, free of his earthly burden and himself. Such is the punishment for sins.
- Well, that's very humane. But if that's the way to get rid of all those who disobey, it won't be long before you and I, my dear fellow, will have to trim the bushes! Hmm.
- No, padre, we'll do it selectively. Ha-ha-ha-ha.

Your laughter is better than old wine to me. That's a good idea, Theo. Don't forget to say the same about the father and his daughter. In their condition, any shock could be their last. Neither of them will outlive the other by more than three days. They will leave their bodies, and their grief-stricken souls will sleep until judgement. "Deus vult," – is the way God wants it. And we serve Him.

Fragment 3
Audience

- I have petitioned the pope himself for you. You will be granted a Papal audience. If all goes well, my dear Theo, you have a great future in a career for the Holy Church. We need men of intelligence and commitment. Your sermon at Campo dei Fiori caused a sensation among the clergy. When it was reported to the Pope, he wanted to see you. The pope's health is failing, so we must think of the future. I hope you will not forget me and become my rival when you climb the stairs in Rome to your happiness. And that will certainly happen, Monsignor Theo and the wait will not be long, I am sure.
- I forget nothing, Your Eminence. Much less kindness. You will see for yourself.

He's sure! He would know how you deal with those who stand in your way or disgust you. He's been watching you for a long time but keeps it a secret on his secret mission. Use it. Especially since he fears you because he doesn't fully know what you're capable of. I don't know that either. Do it, Theo. Do it.

- Monsignor, a letter for you.

Pack your bags, Theo. This message was written by a human hand, obedient to my will. It is the only way I can speak to you. Read it.

"Venerable Brother, I address you with a prayerful request: in the diocese which I govern, events incompatible with the notions of order and piety have been taking place for several days now. A darkness of error and ignorance has spread over the city. Ad rem. It began with the murder of a tax collector by a fisherman named Marco. Today already thousands of unruly heretics, at the instigation of the dastardly Huguenots, pogromed the town hall, the customs house, and the barracks. They have taken up arms and are doing violence to royal and ecclesiastical authority. Many of them have betrayed us. They are in favour of a different faith, demanding the abolition of tithes, lower taxes and threatening to let in troops of foreigners, Satan's collaborators, who are hostile to us. My request to you is that you, with your power of speech and fearlessness of spirit, take part in public preaching to calm the crowd and restore order. Otherwise, we will lose a great deal of land and have an enemy at the walls of our Temple. I know your exploit at Campo dei Fiori, and I admire your courage and faith. Dominus vobiscum (Latin: God be with you). Those of us who hold public weight and power are with you. They plead with me. With luck, my vote at the holy conclave will be yours. We cannot delay a moment longer. I have sent my carriage with guards to fetch you because I firmly believe you will not refuse me, but I remember that all is God's will. Today, you carry as much weight with me as a messenger from Heaven. Your eternal servant, Cardinal M."

A minute later, the three horses were speeding down the cobbled street, driving the frightened passersby away as if Elijah the prophet himself were driving them. Ahead, Theo, you're facing an angry mob of rioters mixed with the fading authority of their leaders, who hate them and fear what they've done. But every one of them is convinced they're on the side of good. I know what you're thinking. Don't worry, they will hear you and believe you. Be firm and no love. To God be God and to Caesar be Caesar. Give them what they want. It's a long journey, you need to take a nap. I'll talk to you because I can't keep quiet. I confess I can be quite talkative. So, what I'm saying is that the division between people leads some to call others "evil" and want to defeat them physically! Oh, foolish ignoramuses! Being darkness themselves, they fight in the darkness with themselves, afraid out of pride to admit to themselves that they are naked and blind. The handfuls of sand taken in both hands are mixed together. Which of them is the winner now that they are one and the same? Sand is like sand, a faceless mass. No matter how much you throw it up, it will all fall down. All these crowds of screaming creatures are to me only instruments of anger of universal proportions. I fear only the bright light that destroys the darkness without leaving a shadow. But as long as you revile me from your wicked hearts, shouting slogans in the name of evil and hatred, that light which I hate will not come and reign. Even en masse, you do not become united, for hatred is blind and impersonal, but hungry and ferocious like a lone weakling lion. It will devour you one by one, because only in the unit, in its uniqueness and exclusivity, there is meaning and significance. And no matter how much you swear to each other in loyalty and devotion to the cause for which you are ready to die, you will never merge together in this hard world! That is the law and the design. You will always be alone, that is why you need meaning. The unit is submissive to temptation: go and take it away. The goal and direction will be given to you by the one who has reached that great and unique unit! This is your leader, this is your god, who first taught you to act on your own, who by his wisdom inspired his wife to pluck and eat the forbidden fruit from the tree of life. He alone has the keys to the gates of the abyss, where everything is constant and abides in its fullness. There, like him, you will attain perfection. But no matter how many times I myself went there to attain the Absolute, the same thing always happened to me: I achieved nothing. Sometimes it seemed to me that it was all just illusion and deception. Yet I tend to think otherwise: my spiritual growth is not sufficient to attain completeness. Being a creature of eternity, I can only change where there is time. But here on earth, I observe the same laws, situations and results happening for centuries. Hence I conclude: there is no time: what was in the beginning, was afterwards, is happening now.

Everything is the same. And the figures are the same. If you look into the soul of a villain, murderer or rapist, you can see there the first day of the fall into sin in its entirety. That very moment of the birth of the universe in man: the division of space into light and darkness. It is like falling into a pit, through the transparent bottom through which you can observe the events and actions of the main characters. And now the climax has come, the day is over and night reigns.

But in the human soul, the night does not end, the dawn does not come. At that moment, when for a moment the light dispels the darkness, there will be exactly nothing. Neither life in darkness nor time without movement has ever been there. A black hole and that's it! And now the most important thing: this most universally despised and dreaded black hole still has a will and a mind! Who dares to say that evil is death? Or nothingness? Nothing can arise from the void. Any villain is very ingenious, very tenacious, cunning and clever. And most importantly, determined. Hence the conclusion: darkness is not the opposite of life, but life in another form. But God does not accept it. Why not? We have arrived. The city gates let out a smell of rotting flesh and foulness. Where I am, it always smells like that. It is nearing noon. Mounted heralds summon the people to the square. Many people envy your stamina and coolness. Your thin lips are set firmly on your dead pale face, shaped by sharp cheekbones and crowned by a low forehead beneath thin, sparse hair. The eagle stare of your frozen eyes penetrates everyone and brings awe to the proud. You don't need to prepare for the speech: I did everything for you while you slept. Be inspired by the image of the coveted goal. Use religion, the name of God, and promise anything. It's done. Their hearts are open. They are hungry for flattery and blessings. My proud spirit will fill them to the brim. Begin.

"O great people, chosen by God and beloved by his Holy Church! My name is Theodore Cossiga. I address you from this sacred place because the time of great revelation has come for you. I cannot be silent! If I keep silent, the stones will cry out! Listen, blessed people, to what I am about to tell you. You have suffered much injustice and poverty in your land for many years. At the same time, you have multiplied and you need more space. Therefore, you are on the verge of despair and are ready to destroy yourself by your own hands. You were led by blind men and rogues, who were ready to ruin you to the last thread and destroy you in a fratricidal war. But the just Lord heard you!"

Now it is not I, but the Lord himself who speaks to you through me. Faithful heirs of a great empire, it is time to remember the past history of your land! If your ancestors were able to make it great, you will be able to do the same! The Holy Church will show you the true path because she carries in her hand the Lamp of God! And in this way, you will earn forgiveness of your sins, find grace, and enter the Kingdom of Heaven as its faithful soldiers! Otherwise, neither external nor internal enemies will ever leave you alone. I am talking about foreigners and sins. The winner takes all! As Christ overcame death on the Cross and gained the whole world, so shall you also gain the new earth prepared for you, which you deserve by right. Who else but you?! You are hired by different lords in their private armies, but the time has come to unite in the one army of Christ. Courage makes for immortality, and the multitude creates strength! Let each of you sell the last of your possessions and buy weapons to secure a better future for your children. Return with victory and feed your children, clothe them, educate them, and entrust their souls to the Holy Church. And God will shed abundant grace on your land and your race. Indulgence paid.

Before, each of you might have died from sickness, drunkenness, or a mean hand, ending up in a ditch or a grave. What would you get from God for that? And where would your soul end up after death? Think about it. No doubt it will be in death's hands. That's why I fear for you, my people!

God wants a different kind of sacrifice! A sacrifice of atonement! Be it today! If you must die, die for something great, with a sword in hand and faith in your heart like a knight! Don't disgrace your ancestors! Every death fills Heaven! Make it so that you do not have to fight the enemy in your own land, that you do not see your house burning, nor the death of your old father or infant son. Did not Christ say, "I have not brought you peace, but a sword"? Your land needs defence, but it does not need fire. So great and blessed nation, go and warn the fire, and keep it away from your house. By doing so you will protect your home from ruin and calamity. It is right to attack, not to defend! Stand on the ground of your brother who is lost in sins, and show him the power of your chivalrous spirit. Reveal to him the truth: "It is the Lord's will"!

Let each of you seek the blessing and guidance of your bishop, and only when you have received it, take up arms and set out on your journey. You have a secure rear. All who can work will work. Whoever is able to take up arms will not hesitate to go and take up arms. The Church and the King are on the lookout for everything. They follow you. Let your thoughts be only of victory. Nothing else matters. The creed of "cross and sword" will be on your clothes, on your body and in your heart. And the battle cry "In the name of God and the King!" will unite you and bring an invisible sword down on the enemy.

On your knees, people of God! I bless you for your holy work! May your sins be atoned for by your works. And grace shall increase in your land. Now your brother's land will also become yours. And he will repent and turn from darkness by your example. And you will shine in the light of the glory of

God, and all the nations of the earth will submit to you like Christ. The truth is with us. We have power with us! "God is with us! Amen."

Bravo, my boy! Nothing too much. The crowd cheers and prays. The choice is made. The darkness thickens around them: God is not here. The light in their souls has gone out. Many of them lack fearlessness and hatred, which seems to them a weakness unworthy of a knight. They have asked for it in prayer. Theo, think about it: they asked the Holy One for hatred of the enemy and fearlessness in battle! And they saw themselves as heroes, parading the glory of the people under His banner! Madmen. They made God an accomplice to their dark deeds! My legions pounced upon them with greed and devoured them. Now they will march for new lands and new companions. Is this not what my lord wanted? Exactly. They want blood.

The deed is done. The reward will be worthy of everyone. And the "reward" will begin today. From now on, none of them will seek the Kingdom of Heaven and its works. They have begun to make their lives here with me. The darkness has set them free. It freed them from the torment of conscience and spiritual tossing between heaven and earth. The enlightened righteous call it "the curse of God." They know well that God has given this world to me. I am an accomplice in his creation but rejected by him because of my right to it. I want revenge. Everyone is capable of loving Him, but not everyone gets that opportunity because of me. I deny the right to exist to all that deny me as god! And even by accepting me as a god, I deny your right to exist as your creator. I deny everything in the universe. This process of denial seems endless to me. This is the "reward" for sin – denying the future. Illusion. Death.

I alone need any religion. It alone is capable of sowing fear into the souls of the living because of insincerity, without arousing resentment in them. Only it is capable of lying for its own benefit without causing refutation. Only she is willing to kill for lack of love without causing opposition. It is possible to love God without her, but to understand His will and know of His existence, is impossible. They began to see and hear only when he sent his son here. He opened their eyes and communicated the Father's will to them. I have never been so furious and angry! Always one step ahead, always stronger, always wiser! I'm blinded by His glory! And yet we were born together. And my mystery becomes as clear as the palm of my hand: such a concentration of darkness in the universe that not a single atom of light leaves its limits. And that puts an end to our dispute for the right to be God: if He creates, I can destroy.

Theodore. I'm furious! I've been set up! Having made the earth round, only He knew that the dawn never ends. And with it, the prayer to Him goes on before the sunset. It never stops! I'm going mad! I'm dying, Theo! I want to swallow the earth whole. Prayer is not prayer, but useless chatter if God is not God! Pray to me and tremble like demons that I leave you alone. A dead man needs no light. Let them pray to you, Theo. Let them obey and fear you, my son. Give peace to their souls. Be the Pope. There must be someone above them. The Son of God has left the earth and we are left in his place. They've already taken up arms and are ready to follow you. You're almost there. Letter.

- His Eminence died this morning. All high clergy, cardinals and bishops, have been notified. Despatches have been sent to the King, the court nobility and the monasteries. The funeral will take place in three days. I've been instructed to prepare the body for a public farewell and burial. The Council of Bishops will meet tomorrow. The date of the holy conclave will be set there. I'm done.
- His Eminence, I understand, left a suicide letter. Do you have it?
- The rescript of his eminence is in the chancery and awaits its promulgation at the holy conclave.
- The letter must not be allowed into the conclave. You will give it to me.
- I have no authority... Wait! Where are you going, Your Lordship? When it comes to the fate of the throne and politics, I am always on the side of the Holy Church.
- More precisely.
- I am ready to give you the letter, but could you in turn reward me with the office of bishop in the lands of my native land? I will serve you faithfully. I am ready to swear an oath!
- We all serve God, my faithful friend. Do not forget that. And I remember that every deed is worthy of reward. Bring the letter to His Eminence's bedchamber. I have an audience with him.
- But, if you please, his eminence cannot receive you, as he is dead...

- Is not immortality promised to every faithful servant of God? Don't be timid, bring the letter. I'll wait for you there. Oh, and a nice glass of red wine, if you please. Or better, two!

My leadership in action. Theodore Cossiga, my boy, history is being written now. And your name is already written in it. The gates of hell are open. Use your greatest advantage, fear. They fear being killed, excommunicated, losing wealth and power, losing their freedom, fearing the scorn and anger of the mob. Your throne will allow you to accomplish and learn much. Most importantly, insist that salvation can only be obtained in the bosom of the Church as a spiritual community, lavishing privileges and titles of bishops or deacons on everyone (as if they had received their authority from God) who wants to call themselves so and pleases you. With His name, enslave everyone who will believe you. Action.

Letter from the late Padre. Time to mock the "righteous." Read it out loud.

"My days are coming to an end, but I am still fluent in my mind and speech. I, Nicolo Poretti, do not attempt to address anyone in particular, for I cannot call a priest a priest, nor can I call you as brothers in Christ my brothers. There is no priesthood or brotherhood left in you. You are inexcusably mistaken in assigning to yourselves and your works the category of divinity and holiness while abusing the illusory power they confer. All your actions are aimed at one thing only: to sow fear and gain obedience of the simple, dark and naive people, as well as of the powerful enslaved by greed and idolatry. You are steeped in selfishness and superstition, not wishing to recognise and glorify the truth, but only substituting concepts and acting in its name. You do not herd the sheep and flock of Christ but feed them to ravenous and insatiable wolves. Is this the kind of Church the Saviour commanded the Apostle Peter? And you call me his successor! During all these years, being at the top of church power, I never ceased to be amazed at how much power I had been given over people! And what amazed me most of all was that I could use it as I pleased. Being a sinner by birth, I did not become righteous on my way here but was only busy pleasing the powers that be, filling the cornucopia, and my vanity, enjoying a supposed holiness. True holiness is out of the question in this form of worship. Every day, while convincing others of the greatness and piety of the sacraments and miracles, I could hardly restrain myself from laughing and wanting to inform them that all this was nothing but illusion and deception. Enjoying eloquence on the subject of infernal torments and heavenly rewards, I justified my conformity to the Throne by helping you to weave a web of deceit and injustice, entangling weak and dark men in it. Today, the very enemy of man and God is ready to take my chair at the first opportunity, and he is already standing at the door, patiently waiting for my death. His name is Theodore Cossiga! Yes, it's true, Theodore Cossiga. Listen to me, lest the Holy Church become a tool in the hands of the devil. It's not too late to change things. Take responsibility and extinguish the infernal flames of lies and hypocrisy that could consume our land and our souls without a trace. After my death, a sacred conclave will elect a new Pope. I pray to God if only he has accepted my sincere repentance and forgiven my sins at my deathbed, to inspire you with truth and prudence, so that you may not commit criminal acts against your conscience, for which you will have to answer in the judgement of God. Do not think that I am motivated by personal hatred or enmity towards this man. No. I know many things about him, but what is most true is that I have not seen a single manifestation of humanity and meekness of heart in his intentions, words, and deeds. "For the tree is known by the fruit." So recognise the tree as bad and its fruit as bad, and drive away the liar and hypocrite! Otherwise, he will demand to be worshipped as a god. It will not happen! There will be found among you a worthy man, a zealous servant of God, who has the mind of Christ, even if I have dared to reproach and rebuke you for your errors and unbelief. Man is not eternal on earth, but our Lord is holy and just in his works and in his judgement. I leave my body and place my soul in the hands of Christ. And at this moment I regret that I did not live my life as a humble, lonely wanderer, whose joy is bread and water, and whose work is to serve my neighbour in love. I die in wealth and luxury, naked and destitute at the gates of Paradise, which are hopelessly closed to me. It's all over.

It's not a wine I'm drinking, but your muddy blood, you silly, noxious old man! You wanted to deprive me of my dignity, and you lost everything. Rise and drink with me, Padre! They've brought us some marvellous wine. But you're immobile and pale because you're deathly ill. Ha-ha-ha-ha! I understand and even sympathise with your grief. And I want to tell you a terrible news: you, Nicolo Poretti, the only surviving son of a poor fisherman, will never rise again, because your God has not forgiven you! And I will take your place after I have honoured you with divine honours and made you equal to God! I am not interested in your opinion on this matter, because I will not reward you, but I will fulfil your "desire." And from now on, so shall it be with every Pope of Rome. Drink with me to that, Nicolo. Swallow your wine quickly. Before, you were not even afraid of blood. Look, it's the blood of the heretics you've executed running down your lips and down your neck and chest. You look like a slaughtered pig in a stable. And you're being very rude to me. You're a plebeian.

And who is the fool who made you pope? Find him and crucify him in the square tomorrow! Publicly! So that everyone will remember that there is only black and white. No compromise! And you're a shining example of that. You were alive and now you're dead. Either for me and with me, or against me and dead. No compromise, Nikolo. No compromise! Do you hear me? I didn't know you were such a good listener. But you're a bad writer, untalented and boring. You shouldn't write letters; you should write denunciations. You don't need talent. You don't have to think either. Let's drink to you! You were the easiest obstacle: you eliminated yourself. Vae victis (Latin: woe to the vanquished). I'll burn your letter. Everything has to be done in time if you want to achieve anything. But you couldn't have done it anyway: you can't see the most important things with your eyes and touch them with your hands. When I was a child, I realised that I was chosen by Providence to do great things. And the likes of you are no obstacle in my way. Sleep well, Nikolo. You've done everything you need to do. Now it's my time. Fight and fight again. Date's over.

Theo Cossiga, I'm saving you for the future. You're part of me now.

Candidate # 2
Scandal

Politics. Making promises doesn't mean keeping them. Blah, blah, blah, blah, blah! But how right and beautifully that son of a bitch Brian Kucharski (Brony) speaks! Only the most honest man lies convincingly. He is honest in that he lies always and to everyone around him, but not to himself. When he finishes his speech and is left alone with himself, he immediately confesses to himself that "today was especially in the blow and achieved the goal." And immediately with one blow he will destroy any doubt: "all these lies are only for the sake of the people, for the greatness and prosperity of the Motherland." What a good man! He was in the right place at the right time. A former officer, and a professional in his field. He has everything you need: a specific goal, a clear mind, a well-positioned speech, a pleasant appearance, middle age, impeccable reputation, and authoritative charisma. I haven't seen anything better in a long time. Except for the little lustful devil hanging around him day and night. Competition? I don't think so. What can a demon get out of you, Brian? Using women to feed your vanity and ego? Or stir up lust to make you dependent on her? How petty it is in this day and age, how banal and old. If it were only about that, I would not pay attention to you and pass by. But the desire to be more successful than others, smarter, better, richer and more glorious attracts me to you in a special way. Plus, it coincides with my ability and desire to express myself in such a multifaceted way. You love power. And its derivatives: wealth, influence, respect, fame. That is the greatness and power of man! And if suddenly a successful man like you is tempted by something or someone and wants to turn to God, God will demand him to give up all earthly goods. In return, of course, he will be promised forgiveness of sins, reconciliation with God and eternal life. But how do we see all this in the mirror? How long to wait? Where to put all these virtues and charisma? To lose is not to gather. Where's the guarantee? Promises are not promises to keep. And if not you, there's bound to be someone else to take your place. There are plenty of competitors. And envious – even more. Why, if the people's recognition has been received, the crowd is cheering, elections are approaching, and there is still time for reconciliation with God?

Things do not wait, things are done. Your reward is known and very great. We will make every trembling creature on earth reckon with us, and then fear us!

Election debates in big politics are always an event. We have a worthy opponent, our equal. He's determined. Don't be afraid, Broni, I'll take the floor tonight. Everything you say is not new and quite predictable: you have been on the pages of newspapers and television for six months. What I'm going to say, however, is not widely known. I brought you to this for a reason. I have an old score to settle with him. It's a challenge.

- Well, we meet again! I thought you were in the underworld behind seven locks. I didn't expect to find you here again. I lost last time by believing you. But I'll be wiser this time. You go first. You're in charge today.
- I will remind you, wretched slave, that my name is the Herald of Delusion! I am made for my desires. Gold and silver serve me. There is no limit to my satiation, otherwise the abyss would not be an abyss. People die every day, but few care where their souls go. In the history of the earth, it's billions. If the abyss had a limit, it would bring back the excess. And its secrets would be revealed. But invariably the abyss wants more and its bosom is not filled. There is a great fire there and something very frightening! That is why delusion has many "doctrines." They are all many faces.

That's why I'm here. And will always be here.

- You changed your name and rhetoric. Why so much pathos? You're concerned with human souls now? You're rich. You want to be among them to justify your need. I trusted you when I set out to build and lead the Empire. But you were jealous of me and wanted to rule yourself. And when I refused to give in to you, you ruined everything. Our long-standing dispute is not over. Today, I am building the Empire anew. My candidate is strong and wise enough. All together cannot control themselves and their destiny, only one can be chosen. I am ready to fight you.

- Fool, everything you built disappeared at first light. You lost, for which you were banished to the Archives. Wasted time and huge sums of money, deceived hopes, and the Empire Building itself fell under the water and now lies at the bottom of the ocean, leaving no trace.
- I built the great Building on thin ice that melted: you lied that the ground was solid. That place you sold me, and assured me otherwise. It was like a dream. I was deluded, but you created Separation.
- Today I am filled with Doubt: do we serve a common cause or is it every man for himself? My spirit tells me to act on inspiration. I took his soul to subjugate the rest. Politics substitutes true greatness for false greatness. Brian Kucharski acts like a church hypocrite in his public appearances: in the temple, he preaches, repents, and prays, and when he walks out the door he curses and sins. His goal is total unqualified power for years to come. Who is your candidate? Have you stooped to these bloody dictators? Are they politicians? They are murderers and rapists; their power is based on fear. Their death is their oblivion.
- I need all human souls so that I can achieve my goal through them. I alone have the right to them, because He said to me, "My patience is only enough for everyone if they repent and convert." I think it would be foolish not to use it. My teaching, "On True Religion and the Struggle against Foreigners," is the most effective at all times. This time the schism is spiritual in nature. There's no shortage of eloquence

here. Religion can turn a man into a beast. But literally, he will not become a beast, but will only accept our image and destiny. Politics is always designed for the masses. Religion unites and politics directs. I'll put them side by side.

- Universality is hindered by lonely minds. They are His voice and His will.
- They're known to me. Each one by name. But I go blind at the sight of them. I will destroy them at the hands of the people. My "Doctrine of the Good of the People" is the simplest of all. It generalises the notion of "the people," depersonalising everyone, and disperses the notion of "good" into the air, imposing its will. My "doctrine" calls "the people" a diverse community whose first "good" will be to get rid of the "enemies" who deny this good. The "good" itself may never exist, but fighting for it is the primary mission of their leader. The crowd listens to him with the greed of a hungry lion, swallowing the lie like a coveted meal.
- Have you learnt to understand and speak like that yourself?
- No, I read their books. They name everything and explain the incomprehensible. You can only fight what is real. If there was no world, there would be no us.
- You know anyone else who would do that?
- No, just man. Adam gave a name to everything he saw with his eyes. But then came one who gave a name to what the eyes could not see. And that only applied to man and those like him.

Who is like a man?

- We are. Before it was the other way round: we were his best friends. And man had no choice until the Serpent tempted him. Only the Serpent knew the secret and was proud of it.
- It's a beautiful tale. I still shudder with fear at the thought that man could have remained immortal if not for the apple. A bitten apple is the substitution of life for death! That is the wisdom of turning man away from the face of God and showing him an idol so that his eyes may be opened and he may realise who his god really is. Intrigue gave birth to action, and action gave birth to self-justification. Real politics! Today, pride gives birth to an idea, an idea gives birth to action, and politics justifies and embodies everything. They love politics. It gives them significance and importance, and often just trivialises their existence. Just like us. I even gave myself a name to make myself seem real. But a person is given a name from birth. Only status comes with time. And I earned my status on my own.
- I'm sick of you, you bore. You've turned this debate into a tearjerker show. Shut your mouth, you hysteric!
- Please behave correctly and do not use insults! We are watched by millions of people!
- I apologise, Mr Moderator of the debate. I've lost my temper as my opponent won't let me get a word in edgewise.

Good for you, change your anger for mercy – the public loves it. Get the dirt out of your pocket.

- Brian Kucharski, the less you are heard, the better for the country! My team found about twenty verbs in your immoral election programme that indicate your future actions. But not one of them is the most important one: don't lie!
- And what exactly do you disagree with in my thesis?
- With everyone.
- That's hypocrisy, Madam former Senator. Many of yours are repeating mine, using the same turns of phrase. You need to start with yourself.
- I hope we're talking about the same country.
- No doubt, but I'm talking about the country of the future. Its greatness and its victory!
- I doubt you can do all the things you have so generously written. Just a moment, let me read out: legislate and enact, protect and protect, improve the system, raise the level, transform, revitalise and shape, reduce and revise, finance and consolidate, restore rights and enshrine guarantees, nationalise and distribute income, equalise and raise wages, cut costs and fight poverty! I think the Lord God Himself makes far less of a commitment to people.
- I get it: you're just jealous of the breadth and depth of understanding of the issues.
- I am ready to have you on my team, Emma, but only after my final victory in the elections.

They laugh, they like you.

- Thanks for the encouragement. But I didn't mean it as a joke.
- Don't you have enough experts on your team, Brian? Or do you have no principles? One goal – power at any cost!
- I know the price you paid, Emma before you found yourself in the senator's chair. I am talking about the meteoric rise from Secretary of the Treasury to Ambassador and then Senator. Did you forget the diamonds? What did the country and its people gain from you holding such an important and high office? How do you deserve to be a senator, Emma? I'll answer that: you bought this post! And I have proof.

Bravo! Intrigue. Passions are running high. The crowd rejoices. The barriers have been erased.

- This is a serious public accusation, Mr Kucharski! Do you have proof?
- No doubt, Mr Moderator. I will provide them at the trial.
- I'll accuse you of lying, Brian! What diamonds? There can be no proof of that. You'll go to jail for slander!
- We are talking about supplying diamonds to China, bypassing sanctions. You worked as an ambassador in the very African country where they were mined and shipped from. I have invoices and payroll records

in my archives. They have your name and your signature. The amount of gratitude for your assistance is enormous!
- That's an outright lie! I never received any thanks! Damn you, Brian!

Good job. You do one thing with me, you're already cursed. One thing is written on paper, but the reality is quite different. Who is the author of the papers? But what difference does it make now? Yes, and her carelessness and ambiguity in the expression "I did not receive any gratitude" will now be picked up and spread by the sensation-hungry media. You can't win with the naked truth alone, my boy. The scandal will do its job: the former senator will have to justify herself, prove her innocence, and spend money and time. And if she succeeds, you will claim later that your enemies wanted to set you up, but you didn't believe the accusations against her until the last moment. Each of you has a flaw, and more than one, but who will stand up for you to turn? Remember: the fullness of all things will never come.

Tomorrow you will have what you have today! If you don't love God, I can do anything for you. But I have always been hindered by His love for you. When you remember that, then you will realise that it is useless to respect evil. The golden idols are gone. Now they worship you and your wealth: they serve you; they pray to you; they glorify your name and your cause. Brian Kucharski, I will preserve you for the future. You are now a part of me.

Candidate #3
Fragment 1
Deal

Thirty coins, the price of blood! The culmination of human greed. Had Judas forgotten that he was mortal? Outwardly the money was necessary to justify the deed, but it was not the purpose. Envy of greatness and power, fear of his own nature of nothingness, must have received at least some compensation. Envy of riches and glory, jealousy of God and the future possessed Judas entirely. The poverty of the Robbers had originally appeared at the same moment when the inhabitants of the higher divine world, in view of their pride, were cursed and thrown down to the earth to wander. They had memorised their former way of life and were now searching for it on earth. It remained in their heart. If they had not become beggars, they would not have become Robbers. The like needs the like. In the same way, the material body needs material satiation for all its desires. In view of their oblivion, they believe that they are still immortal, so they use their time of life to seek and accumulate treasures that exude lustre. This is the easiest and most pliable category of villains I've had the pleasure of working with. Why villains? Because they are never interested in the consequences of their deeds. The most selfish category of earthly beings. They were the first to bow down and swear an oath to the devil to be guaranteed immunity. My best candidates for power.

In the Archives we found the case of one Mark Lamm, nicknamed "Credit." Ambitious and vain by birth, from a young age he had been looking for a way to enrich himself. Once the thought of living a life of poverty and want frightened him so much that the least he was willing to do in the future was to erect a temple in his honour and sit on a throne within it. Starting out in underground casinos and pawnshops, he grew to become a significant banker and investor with a tarnished reputation. His poverty of imagination, earthiness of mind and complete lack of aesthetic taste as a result of his criminal activities created a somewhat different picture. By building a marble palace on the seashore and decorating it with gold and precious stones inside and out, Mark aroused the malicious envy of the heirs and immortal brothers of Judah. Those skilfully bought his inner circle and eventually divided all of Mark's property among themselves. He had to start from scratch again. Now absolute power became his main goal. He saw in it not only a limitless increase of capital and a lot of opportunities but also, most importantly, a guarantee of security of everything and everything. Mark, you'll get everything you want, but I'll take your freedom away from you. Your will only appear to be your will. Matter will completely absorb you, and you will never escape from its shackles, you will never stop, because it lives only in movement, absorption and destruction. Setting ambitious goals, you will move with her only forward and only towards death. And you will never think of anything else, and you will always be lacking. You were and are a pathetic excuse for a human being, Mark. And now I will easily possess you completely.

More than a year ago. The press is abuzz: "A new gold deposit has been discovered in Western Australia! This event stands out because, for the first time in history, a private entrepreneur hired freelance scientists and created a team of engineers to develop a revolutionary new method of searching for gold deposits in the soil at depths of up to 100 meters. Six months of hard work yielded results: the Dungas deposit found is believed to have a gold reserve of 250 million ounces. Approximately 3% of the world's gold reserves are located here! The technology for finding valuable minerals is patented and recognised as the best to date. The lucky owner of a unique deposit attracts the best investors from all over the world. The shares of MLQ-Geology company of the famous former banker Mark Lamm are growing in value every minute! Many big players in the natural resources market are trying to take a bite out of the pie, making the project itself even more expensive and attractive. B&Q Corporation, the world's largest mining company, is ready to become the main partner and the main investor, ready to assume all necessary obligations to MLQ-Geology. Such important news cannot go unnoticed. Follow the events with us!" You are at the pinnacle of glory. But the goal has not yet been reached.

About a month ago. Yeah, that day, Mark Lamm, you were my best student. On the front page of the newspapers: "A major scandal in the gold mining market! As a result of a thorough review of all data and an audit, independent experts have concluded that the Dungas deposit is not a deposit and that there is no gold there at all. The shares of MLQ-Geology, which had a value of 5 billion, plummeted to zero on the day of the experts' conclusion. The legal department of 'B&Q Corporation' sues Mark Lamm and his team for the damage caused to it, which is estimated at 3 billion US dollars. The actions of the main figure in the scandal are considered fraudulent, and the company itself – a financial scam. In case of conviction by the court, according to a well-known lawyer who commented on the event, Mark Lamm faces up to 5 years in prison and a fine of at least $100 million. Follow the developments with us." End of story.

Yesterday. A short press report: "The head of MLQ-Geology Corporation and the main person involved in the case of the false Dungas gold mine in Western Australia, scandalous banker Mark Lamm, disappeared without a trace from his suburban Miami home. It is learnt that at 11:00 am local time today, Federal Marshal John Allen brought a subpoena for the bankruptcy of the Lammled MLQ-Geology, but found no one at home. The incident was immediately reported to the U.S. Department of Justice. Mr Lamm, who was under investigation, was known to be under house arrest and therefore was not allowed to leave his home until the court's decision. At this time, Mark Lamm's whereabouts are unknown. He is wanted by the Federal Court and all necessary authorities have been notified. A court seizure has been placed on his $150 million bail. Stay tuned for more updates. Stay tuned." Escaped.

Today. Your gold mine turned out to be a bluff. You invented it to defraud investors, raise a lot of money and run away with it, throwing everything down the drain. You succeeded in many ways: the money you stole is enough to start a new life and a new business. You have thought of and prepared everything in advance: the documents are ready, the money has been laundered and cashed, and your friends are waiting for you. Shattered faith in a person means nothing to you. My reward for you is a new case on the way to the main goal. And the coveted mountains of gold are in the imagination of all those insatiable bigwigs. You made them. That's the way of the world. It's either you or you.

My way of thinking is becoming more popular and more substantive. I exist and act in a reality that doesn't exist. In a virtual fucking world! In nothingness. The lie as such was born here and has never left its confines. Otherwise, everything in the universe would be true. And I wouldn't even have been born. How does that feel? All of us here are someone else's creations. So the lie is necessary and important. It tries to change reality, to intervene in the past for the sake of the future, but always in vain. That's why it lives very little and inevitably dies. It is very much like a human being! If you look in-depth, the lie is born with him. For example, a man who is born sees only with his eyes and believes what he sees. And lives then only to see with his eyes what he dreams of or desires. And as soon as he sees it, he rejoices and again wants more and better. So the lie walks beside him all his life, whispers its truth in his ears and laughs in his eyes. And no man cares about what is hidden from the eyes. Even if the mind realises that what is hidden from the eyes is a hundred times more important!

"Mark Lamm is a thing of the past. Now you're Fred Keating, investor, philanthropist, founder and CEO of VEK&Co, a new player in the cryptocurrency market. You created an exchange out of thin air." For that matter, so did the new "Fred Keating." You tightened the skin on your face, let go of a small beard, made your skin swarthy, put in contact lenses and changed your hairstyle. You're unrecognisable now. Yes, you have many faces and names! You've become as fictitious as the founder of Bitcoin and his electronic money. What does it matter what kind of money: the passions around it are still the same, human ones. You now have absolute power in the crypto industry. You can dictate the terms of the game; your possibilities are limitless. In one year, you'll increase your fortune by $4.5 billion. But you'll want more again. We'll make a deal. You and me. All the money in the world will no longer be a means to an end. It will become virtual. And then you can control it. Through this door, you and I will enter a world of absolute world power! Power over people! They want what you want: more money. Everyone here wants money. Share your share with them. Recognise that they are stronger because there are many of them. But that doesn't mean they are different. You've already won!

Fred Keating, I'm saving you for the future. You're part of me now.

Fragment 2
Thirst

My time has come. Our goal: to reclaim the planet and everything on it, inside and outside it. The need to prove and argue is a thing of the past. It's time to give back. Few people know where it all began. Much less what it started for. In short, we were cast out of heaven to earth, and we became spirits on earth, hiding from the light in the darkness and eternally tormented by the thirst for satiation. But what can a spirit do without a body in the material world? It needs flesh. Many different kinds of flesh. Some have decided that by subjugating man, the evil spirit, out of pride and enmity, deliberately steals him from the Creator. No, no! No one even thinks about that. I solely enjoy watching human flesh satiate my thirst! I will leave her after I have used her. And she will long remember and mourn me. Surprisingly, my desires match her capabilities. If it were otherwise, I would have passed on. And let anyone now say that man has more than one Creator with me! What is a man better than I? Can I enter where the light is? Never! So the godless man lets me in and is even proud of it. With me, his life becomes brighter and richer, and my existence finds justification and use. I'm not such a terrible villain, as it turns out. Or maybe not a villain at all: demand creates supply. And here I am. Praise me!

Collage of evidence. A little bit of everything for clarity of understanding of the issue. Capital city, metropolis, ancient city. This is where I'll make the most of my time and where I'll ascend to Olympus. Whatever bad things they say about me, I honour tradition. It's Halloween, I'm gonna have fun with them, especially laughing at their idea of death. Silly costumes and masks, lots of fire and noise… Anything is allowed tonight. But that will all be tonight. The day is just beginning, I'm hungry and angry as a lion, so I need somewhere to stay.

Where's that stench coming from?! At the back of the courtyard of an old two-storey house is a rubbish dump. Obviously, it's not clean. I'm sure I'll find a suitable body in one of the rooms that's dejected or depressed. Young man, marvellous. The room is filthy and messy, smelling of dirty laundry and mould. You've been sitting at your computer for a long time with a detached expression on your face, you haven't had breakfast or washed your face yet today. What are you so busy doing? You're looking at the pictures from last night's party, but let me take a closer look: everyone's having fun, but you're sullen and sitting on the sidelines. I know you didn't care enough, you wanted to spend time with them in a different way. Banal fun and dancing, cheap alcohol and pot don't appeal to you for a long time. You have dirty thoughts, but you don't know how to start and you're afraid of something. That's not enough for me. There's a noise in the kitchen… You got a little scared.

Who's in there? Sounds like your mum. She is a very obese lady in a greasy apron, cooking breakfast for you and herself in smoke and stench. She's a slave to gluttony and terribly stupid. She also has a bad temper, and you are about to get a scolding and a few curses because of the dirty room and your idleness. She doesn't know yet that you've been expelled from college for truancy and more. During her scolding, you can hardly contain your anger. You hate her, yourself and your fate, thinking you are a failure and a freak. What do you think of most often? You wish her immediate death, you dream of getting out of this dump and doing something that will prove to everyone that you are a very cool and brave, smart and lucky superhero. I agree, that fate is unfair to you. It won't be long before she's sure to walk into your room to humiliate you again. How dare she do this to you? She doesn't even know who you are! Being a lowly person herself, she's teaching you how to live! Bitch! Animal! You're miserable because of her. Never, never been loved! Never been heard or understood. If anyone ever cared for you, it was your flesh: fed, clothed, a place to sleep. Sometimes you think dogs are loved more. Your mother has threatened to throw you out of the house more than once, Adam. Leo in Cavea (latin: A lion in a cage) What have you got to lose? What are you waiting for? When she finds out about college, he'll do exactly that! Fortune favours the brave. Kill her. It will take time for the police to find the body in this stench. Run away, then run away. You will be avenged. Weapon's in the drawer under the table. Turn the music up... She comes in, comes over, bends over you, swears at you... Shot! Fell down, lying there, moaning... It's done! Bullet in the stomach, lots of blood. Don't look at her for so long. Forget who she is, it's just a dead body now. Pack a few things, take the gun and the money, and go. The day has only just begun.

You can't undo what you've done. You're not the first. There was no way out. Reward will find a winner. Adam, on the street, acts natural, don't draw attention to yourself. Chat with your friends and find out where you're going tonight. Go to a tattoo parlour and get whatever tattoo you want. Death is multifaceted. Your body is your business. While you're at it, we'll figure out a plan of action.

It's dark, and Halloween is starting. You've prepared yourself: you've bought drugs and rented a flat. A large crowd had gathered. Twice as many girls. Tonight, they'll be yours, just like you dreamed. You're pale, you're visibly shivering, so offer them all a drink on you at the disco bar. The alcohol will calm you down. They're happy, marvellous! Gather the most important and inform them that there are heavy drugs for one time (free) and free accommodation with food for the night. And one condition: drugs only after the orgy. It's all grown-up. Let them pass it on to the others. Don't worry, they will not refuse: each and every one of them almost daily proudly reminds their parents that they are adults, smart, know everything, are able to make decisions and stand up for themselves. Where can they go now? Today it is possible to prove it to yourself and others. Especially since alcohol has chased away the remnants of fear. Agreed? Good. Come on, let's go to the pleasures!

Orgy. No shame, no inhibitions, no barriers, no promises. The formerly loving couples suddenly forgot about each other. All the heated bodies wished to merge into one. They surrendered to lust and pleasure, poisoned by voluptuousness to the point of unconsciousness. Where's that formerly unapproachable Christy who wouldn't even sit next to you, Adam? Today you've taken her several times at her own will.

All barriers were erased, the familiar speech was replaced by vulgar speech, and many creatures like me heard and responded, and then came and found suitable bodies for themselves here. With their arrival, debauchery reached its peak, with the result that same-sex "love" seduced and conquered each of the participants in the bacchanalia! My semblances have no gender, they need the passion and intoxication of chaos. But the climax of the celebration is yet to come.

Escaping from reality is possible and necessary. Heavy drugs are meant to finish the job. Many of the "friends" are doing it for the first time. Some are very afraid. They don't even know what they are doing it for. Just like I don't know who else exists besides me. I am only remembered and hindered by the one who is secretly watching me and making me write all this. I am eternal and beginningless. Calm them down, tell them you've calculated the dosage accurately. Do it first, make fun of the cowards. Everyone has to take communion. I'll help you calculate everything correctly… Silence. How young they all are! Good for you, Adam. Nothing good awaits you in life anyway: you've already ruined your soul. Your case is closed and archived. So die with them, Adam! Go to hell, my silly boy. We herd out, we've got better things to do. I helped you as I promised. Dictum – factum (Latin: said – done). I don't need you anymore.

Clerk

I hate order of any kind. Even when I see a whole standing building, I get satisfaction when it is destroyed. I look at a man and remember whose likeness he is. I immediately want to tear him apart. When I humiliate or defile him, I rejoice and exult. Working in the Archives brought pleasure in human baseness and weakness before what is called "sin." And the bigger and stronger the sin was, the more often I stamped it with "damned." It was a bit like a graveyard. Every file in my archives is a story of death. But it's a mystery. I intend to prove that the man is irretrievably lost and not worth a salvific sacrifice. He should be left alone and allowed to do as he pleases with impunity. And everything will fall into place.

And everything will fall into place.

"As long as humankind lacks one common idea and shared unbreakable values, it walks in darkness and stumbles, sometimes causing irreparable damage to itself. There is no need for division and strife, for hatred and bloody revenge against each other. People are born and called to live on earth and only on earth. This is the way the world works. The planet Earth is very small and fragile to torment it with wars, to devastate it with endless spoils and to litter it with tonnes of rubbish. It is our home, and it is time for us to clean it up, put it in order and live happily. And this is possible only when we are one when we all work together.

Our ancestors fought endless wars because they put up borders. Well, what if there are no borders at all? Who would fight with whom and for what?! And even if you have a different skin colour, a different language, habits and traditions, even if you think differently and value other things, all this will not be a barrier to Universality in the near future. I am introducing a new term – "Universality." It is the unity of everyone and everything, what exists on planet Earth. Your skin colour and appearance have a right to be as well as the diversity of flora and fauna, the uniqueness and multiplicity of which brings delight and amazement to everyone who is able to see and admire. We have learnt to combine and combine the diversities of all things, science has succeeded in synthesising the formerly disparate into one whole, the formerly whole into diversity. The system of sounds and signs that we used to call "language" will no longer be a barrier to human communication and cohesion. There will be one perfect language for all. We will create it anew! We will enrich it with concepts, words and phrases from all over the world and introduce a unified system of signs and symbols. Such a level of understanding and coherence has never been seen before on earth! Your culture, customs, and authenticity did not make your ancestors happy and free. Surrender your past to the museum, and open the door for the future!

And now the moment has come when you have come to understand every person on earth, but now you do not know what to expect from him! Therefore, Law and Morality are very necessary – only one unified for all. Only they are just and humane! Only the Law and Morality are indestructible and hard as a stone! And the power derived from them – the guarantee of universal equality! But I can already hear my opponents shouting: we have different values, our own morals and our own faith! I answer without hesitation: you are mistaken! There are no true values other than human life, freedom of speech, the right to work and deserved rest, state assistance and faith in God! The last concept is especially important because it is not the national language, borders or distances that have divided the world, but religion! The world has become blind and dark only because people have decided that each of them has his own Creator who loves them alone on earth. Don't you have two arms and two legs? Or are you from another planet? The time of delusion has passed. There is an epiphany! Henceforth comes the kingdom of Truth: one God for all, one Creator, one Father, and his love is one for all without measure or hypocrisy! There is no one else but God, and we are all his children! Let us do without the chosen "sons", "prophets" and "wise men" of different colours. It is they who have created centuries of chaos and division among people for many centuries. Let there be only one world, one nation, one God! Let us give thanks for everything created by Him and for ourselves on special days of universal Worship. Let us worship not in temples and buildings, where the elite of godless people, who built them, go, but in the temple of living and eternally new nature, created by God. This is just and right. We will be unanimous in our faith and there will be no one left who will still be wrong and think otherwise. One World Religion – minus another reason for enmity, and a firm step towards common values and common morality.

Now I ask you: How much does bread cost in America or Russia? Will the price be the same? No, for two reasons:

because of the different costs and the different currencies. What do we need that for? Let's make one currency and one price for everything! It will make the work easier. Now I want to ask you for money for a taxi so that I can get home in the evening to my wife and children. Every one of you will no doubt not refuse me and donate a note of money for me. I shall be most grateful to you, but my suit has no pockets! Where will I put your generous investment for my journey home? You're right! Cash is obsolete. It's become a pile of rocks in our pockets. Now it's going to be different: A One World Bank of Electronic Payments! One currency for all! Every financial event is now of global significance. One universal monetary system for all with multiple levels of protection and no right to fail! Everyone will be his own Bank and banker in it. Money will make money for the benefit of everyone on earth, not just individual hopelessly greedy beings, as has been the case in the past. Complete control and transparency of the global financial system. Cash and precious metals will be destroyed with no right to resurrection. Trust will now be the key to wealth and success. The age of inclusiveness will leave no trace of the past!

Yes, I repeat, it is Trust! And it is now more precious than gold because the Universal must be managed. To whom would you entrust your present and future? I can't hear you. Me? You shouldn't be so rash. Well, thank you for your trust. But I am but a mere mortal man and I alone cannot carry such a huge and responsible burden. I have only been given the task of designing the idea of Universality, the time for which has come. Therefore, I realise that we humans are not capable of managing and creating such a global world order on a planetary scale! Enough of repeating the mistakes of the past, it is time to learn from the history of our ancestors. They suffered a lot but achieved little. Therefore, we need a single universal System of management, control and distribution of everything that exists and can be accounted for. No "human factor," corruption, fatigue, injustice and omission. Artificial Intelligence can and will fulfil the task set before it, never getting tired and never making mistakes because it was created by people primarily for this purpose. All the best, created and acquired by mankind for all the time of its earthly history, we will put into it as a programme. What can be fairer and wiser than a cold, unbiased intellect that has no hypocrisy? Will he intrigue with himself or lie to himself? This is how "politics" as a phenomenon will disappear from our lives. Vanity and hypocrisy will no longer feed on human gullibility and stupidity. Human vices, as we know, are not peculiar to the machine. But man still reserves the right to customise, improve and control it. This will be done by taking into account the opinion of every free person living under the Law of Generality.

Ladies and gentlemen! We are one step away from the dream. But the final battle is the hardest. The idea of "Universality" must consume the entire world. The experience of the coronavirus COVID-19 has shown that in the presence of a common uncontrollable threat, a previously divided world can unite. And as a result, win! Is there one threat for everyone today? Undoubtedly, everyone knows it – it is a world nuclear war! I will not talk about its consequences. They are obvious. But I will say that mankind has no other way to avoid its own destruction. Universal control of weapons, followed by their total annihilation, is the main goal of "Universalism." And the last, perhaps.

Everything else will be transformed and will take its place in the evolution of the System. The knowledge and experience of Earth's history is quite enough for a just world order. We are the creators of our own destiny – it is worth accepting! We declare a different war – a war against hatred and injustice! I rely on your intelligence, your experience and your sense of self-preservation. Now is the time for action, gentlemen! We will write about this time in history! And stay alive, and be happier than ever! For the future, "gentlemen!"

My nets are skilfully woven. God does not need them – they need him. I will forbid them to worship the Son: none of them will be saved or fill the Number, so I will rule them forever. And if I lose control and feel the Light, I will destroy everything by their own hands. Nothing has ever been easier for me than to turn one person against another. Especially if they're each holding a weapon.

But something tells me the smart machine will do it first.

Where does that sound come from? They're singing His praises again! I haven't got here yet. If they believe and love, He's among them – I can't get in. I'll howl outside. I'll blaspheme from the heart! "For the sake of the weak, you were weak, for the sake of the hungry you were hungry, for the sake of the thirsty You were thirsty." When was this? Who saw that? Don't make me laugh! You, Lord, ate and slept like everyone else! Not a day's work in three years. Gathered round him the hungry, gathered around him the hungry, the sick and the poor and went round with them to the houses and towns where I used to reign over everything and everyone, disturbing my peace. Show me, Lord, who fears you?! Who follows you today? Or who remembers you, Jesus?! I can turn stone into gold and water into wine as well as you. I can heal, and I can raise the dead. I know the future of everyone who is faithful to me – it's the same as mine. If your work does not follow you, then give it up! The Creator is capable of creating many such worlds. Leave this one with them. I will teach them how to live. Remember our old conversation: you can forget the obvious even when you see it every day. I was talking about death. You asked me to remind them. But they don't remember or think about it because they are afraid and don't understand its meaning. Without understanding the meaning of death, which is inevitable, one cannot understand the meaning of life, which is. How can one understand anything at all without knowing anything? It is enough to know about good and evil, but it is not necessary to know what they really are. I offered you a different life on earth, Jesus. We could have built the Kingdom of Universality when you were among men. We would have erased the boundaries between good and evil, and the Creator would have accepted and loved us again. But you were proud of your mission on earth and rejected my friendship. Were those few worth your suffering? They all fell into the pit. You were with them, but you looked down on them when they were at the bottom. In them, you save and crucify yourself! And again and again, the same story repeats itself: they sin – you forgive everything, they are sick – you heal, they are foolish – you admonish. They are tired of waiting for you, Son of God! Their souls are swimming in standing water. Let's get it over with. Let's assume there's no one left here. Leave me the world and go. If it's destined to die anyway, what difference does it make who destroys it and how? I'll hunt down your righteous and send their souls to you in a very short time. I'll turn over the files to the Archives and burn them down with the world. I promise. None of them will ever know. You'll be pure and blameless as before. Why don't you say something? Is it my fault that I was created differently? I'm as jealous of the Creator as you are. Or let the guns speak? Is it not cruel to do so? Even for me, it would be too much. For years I've been breaking my legs over your righteous men on the way to my own glory. Take them for yourself, and make my path straight. Back off!

The bell spoke instead of you. I gave them no chance to live freely, and they accepted their fate.

Your light in their souls blinded me. I cried out in pain so great that the earth shook and trembled! In many lands, not a stone was left upon a stone. I am losing my sense of time. You are near and you want to destroy me, Jesus! Send me away, imprison me, but don't destroy me. Give me a thousand years to think. I'll go back to the Archives as a statistician and audit the Files. Or I'll turn everything over to you for trial. But where's my reward? I've told you so much, there's not enough time, but he still won't let me go. You're in on it with him. I am filled with anger and rage. No one has ever seen evil in its purest form: its appearance is terrible! I will dissolve and fall asleep in humans for a thousand years. And when it is over, I will voluntarily come to your judgement with them. I know for a fact that You alone are the just Judge! Brrr. I'm leaving, I'm dissolving... But I promise I'll come back!